Good Morning, Lady

Good Morning, Lady

By Ida DeLage

Drawings by Tracy McVay

GARRARD PUBLISHING COMPANY
CHAMPAIGN, ILLINOIS

Good Morning, Lady

Pots! Pots!
I have pots.
Ten cents.

I see a house.
I will knock-knock
at the door.
I will see
if the lady is home.

Good morning, lady.

I have pots.

I have lots
of pots.

I do not want a pot.
I have a pot.

Do you want a pan?

A pan is ten cents.

Yes.

I will buy a pan.

I can bake a cake

in my pan.

I am so happy.

I will make a cake.

I will bake it

in my new pan.

Pots!
Pans!
I see a house.
Good morning, lady.

Go away.

I am Mr. Owl.

I want to sleep.

Pots!
Pans!
I see a house.
I will go up, up,
and knock-knock
on the door.

Good morning, lady.

Do you want a pot?

Do you want a pan?

No.

I have a pot.

I have a pan.

I need a basket.
Yes, lady.
I have a basket.
A basket is ten cents.

I am so happy.
I will go
and get nuts.
I will put the nuts
in my new basket.

Pots!
Pans!
Baskets!
I see a house.
I will knock-knock
on the door.

Good morning, lady.

Do you want

a pot,

a pan,

or a basket?

Do you have some rope?

I need a long, long rope.

Yes, lady.

I have some rope.

Rope is ten cents.

Oh!

I am so happy.

Now I have some rope.

I will do my wash.
I will hang it
on my new line.

Pots!

Pans!

Baskets!

Rope!

I see a teeny-tiny house.
I will knock-knock
on the teeny-tiny door.

Good morning, lady.

Do you want a pot?

A pot is ten cents.

Yes.

I need a new pot.

Here is a pot.
A teeny-tiny pot
for teeny-tiny mice.

Oh, no!
I do not want
a teeny-tiny pot.
I want
a big, big pot.

A big, big pot
is fun, fun, fun
for teeny-tiny mice.

Good morning, lady.
Do you have
a pot?

Yes.

I have a pot.

It is full
of good soup
for you, Father Possum.